For Gemk,

Whose endless supply of ideas and honest critique made this possible.

感謝 Gemk

源源不絕的靈感及誠懇的建議讓這一切成真。

The Vain Vampire

愛照鏡子的 吸血鬼

Coleen Reddy 著

陳巽如、賀鵬 繪

薛慧儀 譯

三民書局

Nobody likes vampires.

They sleep in coffins and drink the blood of people.

But that's not all.

沒有人喜歡吸血鬼。
他們睡在棺材裡，會喝人的血。
而且還不只這樣呢！

3

Vampires never get old. They stay young and beautiful forever.
Because of this, many vampires are very, very vain.
One vampire named Vic was so vain that he was in love with himself.

4

吸血鬼永遠都不會變老。他們青春永駐，而且永遠都是漂亮俊美。
就因為如此，很多吸血鬼都非常非常地自戀。
有一個叫做維克的吸血鬼就自戀到愛上了自己！

Vic loved looking at himself. He loved mirrors.
Sometimes while he was trying to drink the blood of one of his victims,
he would suddenly see himself in a mirror.

維克很喜歡欣賞自己的容貌，所以特別愛照鏡子。

有時候，當他正想吸人血時，會突然瞧見鏡子裡的自己。

He would be so busy admiring himself that he would forget
all about his victim.
His victim would get away but he wouldn't even notice,
because once he looked at himself in the mirror, he couldn't stop.

8

他會在鏡子前忙著自我陶醉，完全忘了他的獵物。
於是他的獵物就趁機逃跑了，但他根本不會注意到，
因為他一旦看見鏡子裡的自己，就捨不得停下來不看呢！

Because Vic the vampire was so vain, his hobby was collecting mirrors.
Actually, it was stealing mirrors. His house was full of them.
Vic even put a mirror in his coffin, so that the first thing he saw
when he woke up was his beautiful face in the mirror.

由於吸血鬼維克是這麼的自戀，所以他的興趣就是收集鏡子。
其實，應該說是偷鏡子啦！他的屋子裡堆滿了這些偷來的鏡子。
維克甚至還在棺材裡擺了一面鏡子，這樣他每天醒來第一眼見到的，
就是自己在鏡子裡英俊的臉孔。

One day though, Vic stole from the wrong little girl.
Val's father had just bought her a beautiful mirror
from Vancouver in Canada.
Vic crept into Val's room and stole her mirror.

然而有一天，維克挑錯了偷鏡子的對象，
這面鏡子的主人是個小女孩，她叫薇爾。
她爸爸才剛從加拿大的溫哥華買了一面漂亮的鏡子給她。
維克悄悄爬進薇爾的房間，偷走了她的鏡子。

But Val heard him.

She got up and silently followed the vain vampire to his home.

She saw him get into a coffin and realized that he was a vampire.

Then she saw all the mirrors and realized that he was a vain vampire.

14

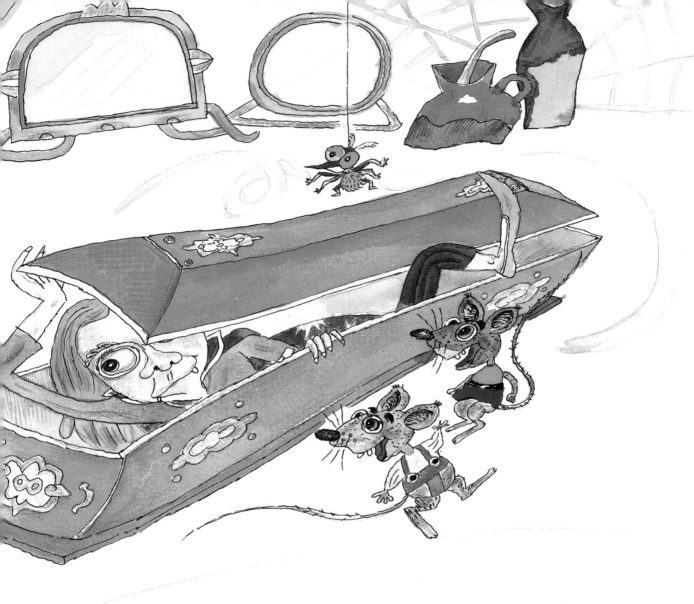

但是薇爾聽見了他的聲音。

她爬起來，偷偷地跟著這個自戀的吸血鬼來到他家。

她看見維克爬進棺材裡，於是知道了他是一個吸血鬼。

然後她看見到處都是鏡子，這才明白，他是個自戀狂吸血鬼！

Val looked for her mirror but she couldn't find it.

The vain vampire had hidden it.

She was very angry. She decided to get even with the vampire.

薇爾到處都找不到她的鏡子。
這個自戀狂吸血鬼把它藏起來了。
薇爾好生氣喔！她決定要展開報復。

She ran home and then returned with her mother's make-up.
Her mother wore special make-up that wouldn't come off even if
you washed your face with water. The make-up would only come off
if it were washed off with a special cleanser.

她跑回家，帶著媽媽的化妝品跑回來。
她媽媽用的是一種特製的化妝品，
擦在臉上後就算用水也洗不掉，
只有用一種特殊的卸妝液才能洗掉。

Val opened the coffin while Vic was sleeping and
put her mother's make-up on his face.
She used ugly colors and made him look really ugly.

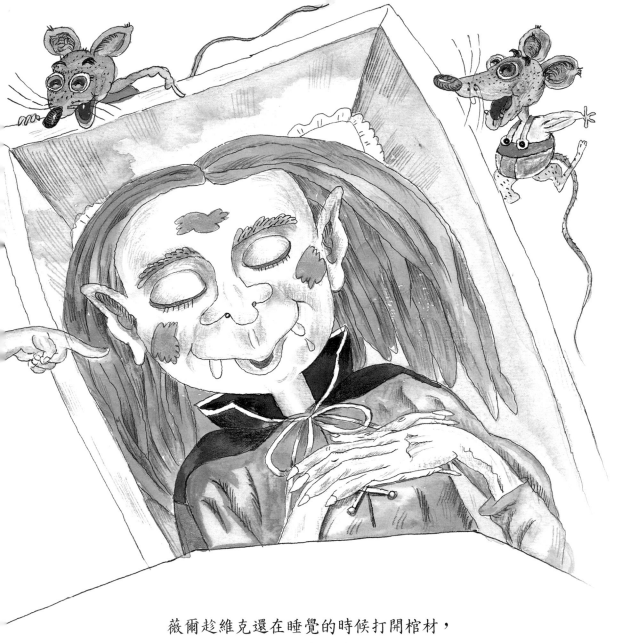

薇爾趁維克還在睡覺的時候打開棺材，
把媽媽的化妝品塗在他臉上。
她用很難看的顏色，把維克塗成一個醜八怪。

Then she wrote a note that read: "I put an ugly curse on you because you are so vain and because you stole my mirror.
I will remove the curse if you return my mirror."

然後她留下一張字條，上頭寫著：「我對你下了一道變醜的詛咒，
因為你太自戀，而且又偷了我的鏡子。
等你把鏡子還給我，我才會把詛咒取消。」

Vic woke up the next night and the first thing he saw was himself.
But oh, it was such an ugly self!

He got such a fright that he screamed.

第二天晚上維克一醒來，首先看到的就是鏡子裡的自己。
喔！天呀！他怎麼變得這麼醜呀！他嚇得尖叫了出來。

Then he read the note that Val wrote.

He tried to wash the stuff off his face but he couldn't.

He really believed it was a curse.

然後他看見了薇爾留下的字條。
他試著把臉上的東西洗掉，但就是沒有辦法。
現在他相信這真是薇爾下的詛咒了。

"How could this have happened to me? Look at my beautiful face!
I'm so ugly. I don't want to live," cried Vic the vain vampire.

「這種事怎麼會發生在我身上呢？看看我俊美的臉！
現在醜成這副模樣！我不想活了啦！」自戀狂吸血鬼維克哭了起來。

But he did want to live.
So he went to visit Val and he took her mirror with him.
Val was not surprised to see him.

但是，他當然還想活下去啊！
因此，他帶著薇爾的鏡子去找她。
薇爾看到他來，一點也不驚訝。

"Here's your mirror! Now take this stupid curse off," said the vampire.

"Okay," said Val. "Close your eyes for a minute."

Val quickly wiped the make-up off the vampire's face with the special cleanser.

「這是你的鏡子！還你！現在可以把這笨詛咒解除了吧！」吸血鬼說。

「沒問題！」薇爾說。「把眼睛閉上一分鐘。」

薇爾趕緊用特製的卸妝液，把吸血鬼臉上的妝擦掉。

When Vic opened his eyes, he looked at himself in the mirror.

The curse was gone.

He was so happy. He was handsome again.

34

維克張開眼睛看著鏡子裡的自己。

詛咒消失了耶！

他好高興喔！他又像從前一樣英俊了！

"What kind of curse was that anyway?" Vic asked Val.
"Oh, it's a curse for vain people," Val lied.
"But it's over now, right?" asked Vic.

「那到底是什麼詛咒呀?」維克問薇爾。

「喔,這詛咒可是專門用來對付自戀狂的喔!」薇爾騙他。

「不過現在這個詛咒消失了,對吧?」維克問。

"No," said Val. "The curse never really goes away.
If you are ever vain again, the curse will come back and
even I won't be able to take it off. You will be ugly forever!"

「還沒有喔！這個詛咒永遠不會消失，
只要你又開始自戀，詛咒就會回到你身上。
到時候，即使是我也沒有辦法消除，你會一輩子都是個醜八怪喔！」

The thought of looking ugly forever scared Vic.
He decided not to be so vain. He sold all his mirrors.
But he couldn't bring himself to take the mirror out of his coffin.
"It's okay to love yourself just a little," thought Vic to himself.

一想到永遠都是醜八怪，可把維克給嚇壞了。
他決定不再這麼自戀了。他賣掉了所有的鏡子。
但是，他卻捨不得把棺材裡的鏡子拿出來。
「只愛自己一點點應該沒關係吧！」維克這樣想著。

41

吸血鬼的傳說

在「愛照鏡子的吸血鬼」這則故事當中，我們知道了一些吸血鬼的特性：睡在棺材裡、喝人的血、而且還青春永駐。你對於這些吸血鬼認識多少呢？讓我們一起來看看一些關於他們的傳說吧！

在很久很久以前，世界上就有很多地方流傳著不同的吸血鬼傳說，大部份來自於歐洲。它們在歐洲流傳了好幾個世紀，使得歐洲人對於這種傳說中的生物往往是又尊敬又害怕。

在吸血鬼的傳說裡，最最有名的就屬「德古拉伯爵 (Earl Dracula)」了，他是吸血鬼的代表性人物。這號人物來自於十九世紀英國作家史托克 (Bram Stoker) 的名著──「德古拉 (Dracula)」。

事實上，德古拉伯爵是真有其人喔！西元十五世紀有一位作風殘暴的弗拉德四世，他的綽號就是 Dracula（Dracula這個名字原來指的是「龍之子」，後來羅馬尼亞人把這個字跟「惡魔」做連結，於是這個字漸漸變成魔鬼或龍的別稱）。他是羅馬尼亞的民族英雄，曾經從土耳其大軍的手中拯救了自己的國家，但是你知道他用什麼方式來嚇跑敵人嗎？他用尖尖、長長的木樁，將成千上萬的俘虜刺死。看到這個悲慘景象的土耳其大軍於是喪失了鬥志。雖然他沒有真的吸人血，不過他殘暴的行為用「吸血鬼」這三個字來形容一點也不為過。

史托克創造這本小說的靈感，就是來自於這位弗拉德四世，而現在我們常常在電影或小說裡看到的吸血鬼，可以說都是根據這部小說中「德古拉伯爵」的形象所創造出來的。

吸血鬼的特性是什麼呢？除了喝人血（或是動物的血）、永遠年輕之外，他們還「見光死」，所以都只能在晚上出來活動。如果他們被大太陽照射到，就會化成灰而死去！（如果仔細看，你會發現故事裡的維克也是在晚上出門、白天睡覺喔！）另外，也有些傳說認為吸血鬼會害怕大蒜、十字架、聖

水和火；還有一種說法主張要用木樁或劍插進他們的心臟，吸血鬼才會真正死去。是不是只要被吸血鬼吸過血的人，就會變成吸血鬼呢？有人認為只要被吸血鬼吸過

血，那個人就會變成吸血鬼；但是另一種說法則認為要喝了吸血鬼的血液，才會變成吸血鬼。

這樣，你是不是對神祕的吸血鬼有了更進一步的了解呢？

生字表

全新創作 英文讀本
帶給你優格（yogurt）般，青春的酸甜滋味！

附中英雙語CD
（共八冊）
適讀年齡：10歲以上

Teens' Chronicles

愛閱雙語叢書

青春記事簿

大維的驚奇派對／秀寶貝，說故事／杰生的大秘密
傑克的戀愛初體驗／誰是他爸爸？
叛逆大維打工記／外星老師來上課／耶！放假了！

你我身上純真的影子，
透過一篇篇幽默風趣的故事重現，
推薦你這套青春無悔的創作系列，
讓愛玫、杰生、大維、凱爾、海倫、傑克，
帶你進入他們的世界，品味另一種學習英語的全新感受。

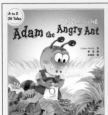

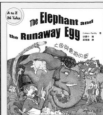

A to Z 26 Tales

二十六個妙朋友，陪你一起

愛閱雙語叢書

✿26個妙朋友系列✿

二十六個英文字母，二十六冊有趣的讀本，最適合初學英文的你！

夬樂學英文！

精心錄製的雙語CD，
　　讓孩子學會正確的英文發音
用心構思的故事情節，
　　讓兒童熟悉生活中常見的單字
特別設計的親子活動，
　　讓家長和小朋友一起動動手、動動腦

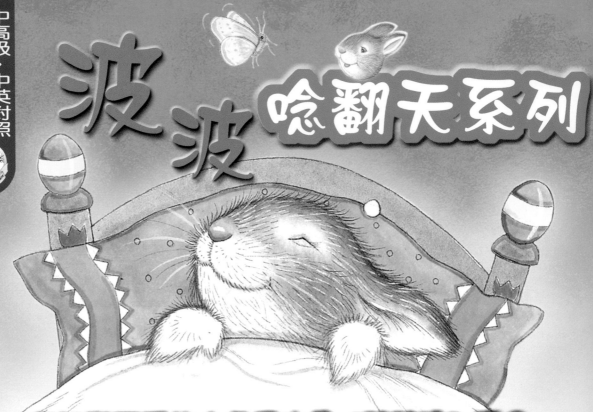

國家圖書館出版品預行編目資料

The Vain Vampire: 愛照鏡子的吸血鬼 / Coleen
Reddy著; 陳巽如, 賀鵬繪; 薛慧儀譯.－－初版一
刷.－－臺北市; 三民，2003
　　面；　公分－－(愛閱雙語叢書.二十六個妙朋
友系列) 中英對照
ISBN 957－14－3757－3　（精裝）

1.英國語言－－讀本

523.38　　　　　　　　　　　92008820

© **The Vain Vampire**
—— 愛照鏡子的吸血鬼

著作人　Coleen Reddy
繪　圖　陳巽如　賀　鵬
譯　者　薛慧儀
發行人　劉振強
著作財
產權人　三民書局股份有限公司
　　　　臺北市復興北路386號
發行所　三民書局股份有限公司
　　　　地址／臺北市復興北路386號
　　　　電話／(02)25006600
　　　　郵撥／0009998-5
印刷所　三民書局股份有限公司
門市部　復北店／臺北市復興北路386號
　　　　重南店／臺北市重慶南路一段61號
初版一刷　2003年7月
　編　號　S 85655-1
　定　價　新臺幣壹佰捌拾元整
行政院新聞局登記證局版臺業字第○二○○號

ISBN　957-14-3757-3　（精裝）